THE BUMPY ROAD TO WEMBLEY

A fabulous football adventure

Pete Barnes

This is a work of fiction. Names, characters, businesses, places, events, locales and incidents are either the products of the author's imagination or used in a fictitious manner. Any resemblance to actual persons, living or dead, or actual events is purely coincidental.

ISBN: 9781980641797

This book is dedicated to my wonderful sons James and Daniel, who are my inspiration for this book and who make me proud every day.

CHAPTER 1

Joy

"**B**oys, for the last time, have you packed your suitcases?" shouted Dad, "we leave in an hour."

No one answered, as usual, so Dad trudged up the stairs and went into the boy's bedroom.

Jimmy and Danny were on their X-Box again, with their suitcases sat empty on the bed. Dad went downstairs, turned off the Wi-Fi and waited.

"Dad, Wi-Fi's down" came a voice.
"Pack your cases, that will fix it" replied Dad.

Dad persuaded Danny that he may need more than his iPad, his Norchester City kit and a pair of pants for a week at his Grandparents!

Cases finally packed, they hit the road, ready for the long journey to Norchester. At least their cousins would be there waiting for them, they thought.

"I'm so looking forward to this week," said Jimmy.

"What time will we be there?" added Danny.

"Around 8 if the traffics ok," replied Dad.

"But I told Nicky on facetime we'd be there by 7," Danny groaned.

Dad pulled the car onto the drive after what seemed like an eternity to the boys. Nicky threw open the front door of his Nana and Grandad's house and raced out to greet his cousins. The boy's Nana and Grandad were equally delighted to see them all, giving each of them a big hug.

Nicky and his older sister Amelia were also in Norchester for the week. The lads were most looking forward to the Norchester City Footy camp that Grandad had bought them as a Christmas present, whilst Amelia was just glad to be away from her nagging parents for the week!

When the boys walked in Amelia didn't budge from the sofa, earphones in, phone in her hand, scrolling through Instagram.

"Hi Amelia," said Jimmy and Danny together. Amelia waved, or it could equally have been a dismissal.

As Nana served up a huge supper, Grandad asked the boys if they were looking forward to Footy camp? Danny jumped up from the dinner table without saying a word, raced upstairs and returned as quick as a flash with his Norchester City shirt, turning it around to reveal 'Murphy number 11'.

"Jimmy's got the other Murphy," said Danny.

"I'd have thought you would have gone for Frank Beefburger," replied Grandad.

"It's Hamburger! Why are you always getting people's names wrong?" moaned Jimmy.

"You will understand one day," answered Dad, "and don't be rude to Grandad" he added.

The boys wolfed down their dinner and simultaneously asked Nana if they could leave the table. Nana knew they had been so looking forward to this week, so agreed,

"Just this once mind."

The boys raced upstairs to get changed into their Norchester City kits before heading outside to play football in the garden.

"But it's dark outside!" Amelia shouted.

"Who cares!" answered Nicky.

Dad, Nana and Grandad finished their dinner with Amelia also at the table, but with her earphones still in, she may as well have not been there.

"England were terrible last night," said Dad, "did you watch it?"

"I did" replied Grandad, as he stuffed a sausage into his mouth.

"And it's the same boring football, same old faces, same old England.   Northgate should take a look at some of the youngsters" he added.

"Why don't you tell him?" asked Dad.

"I might just do that," answered Grandad.

CHAPTER 2

Despair

The England Manager Bobby Northgate sat at his office desk at the Football Association's wonderful training facility, St Georges Park. He stared out of his office window, wondering where the goals were going to come from.

He had just attended a press conference, where the journalists had given him a proper grilling and he felt tired, not just because he was now sixty-five years old, or because he had stayed up late watching match of the day!

Bobby had been England manager for just over a year, having successfully managed teams around the world. He had finally got his chance to manage his country, the greatest honour he could ever imagine. But he had not imagined just how critical and mean some people could be!

England's last match had seen them draw nil-nil with Slovakia, leaving them needing a big win in their last game against their old rivals Germany at Wembley to ensure qualification for the world cup finals. Even Bobby had to admit that he maybe deserved some of the criticism for that draw.

But the supporters, press and football pundits seemed to have forgotten that Bobby and England had been dealing with a massive injury crisis. Bobby had considered putting on his own boots or recalling retired striker Emilia Huskey!

He flicked on his computer which told him he had mail. Amongst all of the adverts and boring FA emails was an email from a 'Mr Barnes', the subject of which read;

'GO INTO THE LOWER LEAGUES BOBBY!'

Bobby was about to delete it as he thought this chap was telling him to step down and take a job at Accrington Stanley or some other lower league club. Then for some reason, he decided to open it ...... and the decision changed his life and football history!

CHAPTER 3

You have mail

The email from Mr Barnes went on to explain that there was a whole wealth of talent outside of the Premier League if Bobby would take a moment to watch the Championship or even League One.

Mr Barnes explained that former England managers always picked the same faces, typically from the Premier League, yet there was such a wealth of talent in the lower leagues if they would only care to look.

Bobby looked thoughtfully out of his office window again, which overlooked the vast training pitches at St Georges Park. He cast his mind back and remembered times over the years when he had also given youth a chance. He remembered that it also seemed to keep the older, more experienced players on their toes.

The penny dropped, Bobby suddenly realised he had become fixated with playing Premier League players and selecting the same old faces, regardless of whether they were playing well or not, exactly as Mr Barnes had said.

Bobby then thought to himself that his current England captain was himself playing in the Championship, having chosen to stay loyal to his sole club rather than take a big money move back to the Premier League when his team were unfortunately relegated.

The email then went on to say that there were two brothers playing at Norchester City called the 'Murphy Brothers'. They were banging in the goals and terrorising defenders in the Championship with their lightning pace, amazing skills and deadly finishing...... yet they were only 17 years old.

Bobby turned to his computer, opened the internet and carefully typed 'amazing Murphy brothers' which brought up lots of results. He was impressed with himself that he had managed to get on the internet at all, as computers were somewhat alien to him. It was his personal assistant Carole who had been teaching him, saying it would open his eyes to new ideas.

Bobby clicked the first link which flicked onto a video, then there was a pause, 'I've broken it', he thought. But a moment later the video launched and went on to show footage of two Irish brothers trying to cross the Atlantic Ocean in a bucket!

"That can't be them!" he cried out loud.

He clicked the second title which brought up the same brothers, this time trying to fly a home-made rocket to the moon.

"Who are these idiots?" Bobby shouted at the computer, as the rocket made from old car parts burst into flames.

"Third time lucky" he whispered as he clicked on the third link. Again, there was a pause as the video loaded, then an advert came on to the screen before finally, the actual video started. Bobby's jaw dropped as he watched the compilation of goals and skills from the two 'wonder' kids.

Bobby picked up the phone and calmly asked;

"Get me those two Brothers from Norchester City!"

CHAPTER 4

Day Trip

Harry Breville shouted out loud for the umpteenth time that day. He had been travelling for 8 hours and had endured a puncture, numerous traffic jams, lots of wrong turns and an incident with some Norchester Town Fans at the motorway services who deliberately blocked his car into its space with their own car, when they saw him head into the services.

Harry was an ex-professional footballer, TV Football pundit and now assistant England manager. He had played under Bobby Northgate and had always done a good job for him. He had surprised everyone in his role as a pundit, with even his fiercest critics having to admit that he was pretty good and talked a lot of sense.

But as a player, Breville was a hard man and was never afraid to get into the faces of fans, players and even the referee! The Norchester Town fans had never forgotten how he waved at them when his team relegated them to the Championship some years earlier, hence why they blocked him in when he answered his call of nature.

When Bobby Northgate got the England Managers job, Harry had called him out on TV and stated what he would do in his position. Bobby had liked what he suggested and soon installed him as his assistant.

The trouble was though, Harry knew almost all there was to know about football, but he was like many other ex-professionals who were used to having everything done for them. He wasn't used to driving long distances, as he would normally have got on the team coach, a plane or been chauffeur driven. So, instead of going to the Norchester City Training ground he ended up at the City stadium!

Harry got out of his car and stretched his legs as he looked at his surroundings. It had been years since he had last been here and then it was as a player. Breville had always played well when he visited Norchester City, so it was great to be back.

But today the ground was deserted, well it would be, it was a Monday afternoon, no match today. Breville saw movement, the club shop was open, so he headed for the door.

He opened it, scanned the shop and picked up a t-shirt which read;

'City till I Die'

with a picture of club legend Frank Hamburger on it. Breville laughed as he remembered a particularly late challenge he had made on a much younger Hamburger! He put the t-shirt back on the rail and approached the counter where a lady stood in the full Norchester City kit!

"Where are the players please?" he asked.

Now it just so happened that there was a kid's footy camp on at the ground that week and that the youngsters were playing on the stadium pitch as a special treat.

Harry was brought up in the north of England, so the lady didn't really understand his strange accent. Breville couldn't really understand her strange accent either, but eventually, with some gesturing, slow-talking and a pen and paper she directed him through into the stands, having understood him to be one of the kid's parents who had come to watch.

Harry watched the training match and quickly spotted the Murphy Brothers as they were wearing Norchester City kits with their names on. They were smaller than he expected, in fact, all of the players seemed very small and there were also some girls playing.

But the Murphy brothers stood out, with their lightning pace, amazing skills and deadly finishing. Breville watched as the two brothers combined to score a superb goal.......

'Just as the gaffer had said' thought Breville. At a break in training, Breville spoke to the lads and gave them a business card with his details on.

CHAPTER 5

St Georges Park

Jimmy and Danny sat on the sofa eating breakfast, playing FIFA on the X-Box and watching their favourite 'YouTuber' on their iPad's. They were making a real mess with their breakfast as they always seemed to do.

"Boys, sit at the table please," requested Dad, but as usual they were so in the zone that they didn't hear him, or more likely didn't want to! Besides, they couldn't play on all their gadgets if they sat there!

Given that they were just 8 and 10 years old, the boys didn't seem at all nervous that they would be joining the full England squad for training at St Georges Park later that day.

Their Dad, on the other hand, was wearing a hole in the carpet, pacing up and down and fussing over them. He had been so excited since the unexpected call from Bobby Northgate about his sons as he knew they were good but didn't realise just how good! He had asked if there had been a mistake but Northgate had insisted that there hadn't been.

"We are leaving in an hour," said Dad.

"But it's only 8 o'clock," Jimmy replied. "And what time do we have to be there?"

"How long does it take to get there?" added Danny.

"Midday and about an hour, but I don't want to be late, traffic could be horrendous for all we know," said Dad.

Dad parked the car, the boys looked at the clock and noticed that it was 10 o'clock exactly.

"Traffic was ok then," said Danny sarcastically!

They sat in the car for an hour and a half before Dad agreed that they could finally head inside.

Jimmy and Danny noticed that the pitches got better and better as they neared the enormous indoor training facility. They strode up to reception where a smart looking lady was typing quickly on her computer. The boys noticed her badge, her name was Carole.

"Bobby Northgate please," Dad said politely.

"He's rather busy today," answered Carole. "He's got a press conference this afternoon" she added.

"Ok then," replied Dad, "Harry Breville then please, tell him the Brothers are here and we are expected."

Carole sighed, more autograph hunters she thought, but she dialled Harry's number and was surprised to hear him say;

"Great, I'll be down in 2 minutes."

CHAPTER 6

Sorry Gaffer

Harry Breville greeted the boys with a warm friendly smile and welcomed them to St Georges Park. The lads had chosen to wear their new Norchester City kits which both had the name 'Murphy' on the back, the same shirts they had worn for the footie camp the week before.

Harry Breville guided the boys down the corridors of St Georges Park, as the lads gazed in awe at the pictures on the wall of their heroes. There were also lots of pictures of older players that they didn't recognise. They passed a wall which had written on it in foot-high letters;

'You have a better chance of winning as part of a team than as an individual'.

Breville ushered the lads into the changing room, sat them down in a spare place and went off to try and find them smaller training kits as the ones hanging on the pegs would clearly not fit them. Carole sent him to the St Georges store where he had to buy two junior England kits with his own money!

Danny and Jimmy sat amongst the players and looked around at the faces they were so used to seeing on TV.

"Alright, I'm Jimmy and this is my brother Danny" pointing at Danny who was a little star struck, to say the least.

Frank Hamburger was first to speak, saying;

"Norchester City fans then lads" with a big smile on his face.

Second to speak was a huge man, sat in the corner;

"Should have worn a Norchester Town kit if you ask me!"

Hamburger was not only the England captain, but he was captain of Norchester City and was Danny's favourite player. The voice from the corner belonged to John Smelly,

Norchester Town's no-nonsense defender and also the England Vice-Captain.

The room fell silent as the door swung open and Bobby Northgate, the Gaffer, walked in. He was a little surprised to see two youngsters in the changing room, but shook each of their hands, thinking that they must be one of the player's kids.

He carried on with his preparations, scribbling some notes on the whiteboard. The door opened again, this time it was Breville, carrying a plastic bag with the England logo on.

"Have you met the lads yet?" he asked Northgate.

"Yes," said Bobby "but we need to get started so best get them out of here shortly. Which players kids are they?" he added quietly.

"Eh Gaffer?" Breville replied looking very confused.

"Oh and are the Murphy brothers here yet?" Northgate asked.

"Yes, they are sat right behind you boss and I've just had to buy them a kit each out of my own money" whispered Breville sounding very confused, holding up the receipt.

Bobby Northgate grabbed Harry Breville by the arm and led him out into the corridor.

"Sorry Gaffer," said Harry, as he tried to explain about the puncture, the traffic jams, the Norchester Town fans blocking his car in and the funny speaking lady in the club shop.

"I get all of that but how on earth have you mixed up the amazing Murphy brothers with a 10 and 8-year-old!" bellowed Northgate.

"But you spoke to their Dad," Harry replied.

"I did, but I just told him we wanted his sons to come and play for England! Now I know why he was checking and double checking!" Northgate snapped, sounding increasingly annoyed. "Their Dad is going mad out there," he added, "he is saying he will go to the papers, the TV and will make it go viral!"

Bobby thought back to his recent activity on the internet, knowing how much damage could be done and how quickly news good or bad could travel.

"You know what? I think I'll just let them train," he said, "after all, what harm can it do?"

CHAPTER 7

John Smelly

John Smelly picked himself up in a daze. He had just been mugged off by an 8-year-old who was not even meant to be training. The double drag back had left the England Vice-Captain completely bamboozled and feeling dizzy.

Meanwhile, the established and experienced England centre-back Glen Molehill was still trying to work out what had happened after the 10-year-old had shouted;

"PANNA"

and then casually put the ball through his legs.

Bobby Northgate and Harry Breville watched from the side-line as the Barnes brothers made mincemeat of the England team. England's right back Carl Runner was quick, but Jimmy Barnes was quicker. Leighton Beans had a sweet left foot, but Danny Barnes' was sweeter.

Undoubtedly the highlight of the training match though was when 8-year-old Danny Barnes rainbow flicked the ball over the England Playmaker David Wickham straight to his 10-year-old brother. He promptly controlled the ball on the edge of the area, did the 'elastico' on Wickham and then dinked the England keeper Joe Fart as he rushed out to smother the ball only to see it lifted over him.

The fringe players with the Barnes brothers beat the first 11 England team 8-1 with the boys each grabbing a hat-trick and an assist!

"HAVE YOU COMPLETELY LOST YOUR MIND?" a journalist asked as Northgate and Breville announced their squad for the friendly match with Wales.

"AN 8-YEAR OLD AND A 10-YEAR OLD!" another shouted.

Back in the changing room, there was a mixture of embarrassment and excitement as the England Squad watched the two wonder kids doing keepy-ups with a pair of John Smelly's pants as he tried unsuccessfully to snatch them back.

CHAPTER 8

Rewind

"So, who exactly are these kids?" asked one of the many journalists.

"Probably best if I let their Dad explain," said Northgate.

The boys Dad took his seat alongside Northgate and Breville looking very nervous. He was not used to public speaking. Northgate introduced the boys Dad to the assembled media. As the photographers snapped away two youngsters at the back of the room laughed as the flashes from the cameras seemed to make their Dad's head seem shinier than normal.

"So, who exactly are these kids?" the same journalist asked again.

"Where are they from?" shouted another.

"What makes you think they are good enough to play for England?" asked a voice at the back of the room.

Dad took a deep breath and spoke softly;

"Why don't I start at the beginning" ......
He explained that the two boys simply loved football. When they weren't playing they were watching it, talking about it, or more than likely dreaming about it.

Jimmy was the older brother, at 10 years old, with Danny the younger of the two at just 8 years old. He went on to outline that they lived just an hour or so away from St Georges Park in the Midlands and were terrorising defences across the region, albeit at their own age.

The boys Dad went on to explain that thankfully the lads were both Norchester City fans like him and that they were spotted playing at City's ground by Breville whilst they were on holiday with their grandparents.

He didn't reveal that Breville was in fact meant to be watching the Murphy brothers, realising that such knowledge could not only jeopardise the boy's selection but that it would also make Breville and Northgate look even more foolish than the journalists thought that they were by selecting two kids. Given that the lads had always dreamed of being professional footballers he did not want to ruin their fairy-tale.

Breville and Northgate were also mightily relieved that he had not told the whole story!

"So, you think they are good enough?" asked a journalist again.

"Maybe you ought to ask Fart, Wickham, Beans, Smelly or the captain Hamburger," answered Dad, now sounding far more assured.

"Are they even old enough?" asked another journalist.

Northgate knew the answer as he had used his new best friend, the internet, to find out for himself. He explained that whilst they had to be 16 to sign as professional footballers there was, in fact, no ruling as to what age they had to be to play international football. The reality was that no kids of their age anywhere in the world had ever been considered for selection by their country as there had never been any kids of their age that were considered good enough.

"Just time for one more question," said Northgate.

"Yes, you at the back," he said looking at the small raised hands (Just like at school, Danny and Jimmy had both raised their hands to ask a question).

"Err, do we get to keep our kits?" asked one voice.

"What numbers will we wear" asked the other.

"Actually, I'll need the kits back" interrupted Harry Breville, looking through his wallet for the receipt.

CHAPTER 9

The Debut

Jimmy and Danny argued for most of the coach journey about who had the best left foot, Danny or Gary Hay-Bale, the Wales skipper and superstar. Eventually, Bobby Northgate had enough and separated them, making Jimmy sit next to Stevie So-Hard and Danny with the keeper Joe Fart.

Fart couldn't believe how much Danny knew about the Wales team, saying;

"You must watch loads of matches."

But the reality was that Danny and indeed Jimmy's football knowledge actually came from playing FIFA on the X-Box and was little to do with watching actual matches. Danny told Fart that Gary Hay-Bale always put his penalties to the keeper's right. John Smelly overheard Danny and Joe's conversation, shouting;

"That big Jessy is not getting a penalty from us!"

Meanwhile, Jimmy got moved again, this time for upsetting midfielder Stevie So-Hard, after apparently giving him a wedgie!

The Millennium Stadium was packed to its 72,500 capacity, though the boys didn't seem at all concerned as they tried to hit the crossbar from the edge of the area whilst all the other England players did their pre-match stretches.

"Kids know no fear at that age," commented the TV presenter Gary Vinegar as he and the other pundits discussed the match.

"I've said it before and I'll say it again, you'll win nothing with kids!" replied one of the other pundits.

International Friendly Full-Time Score

Wales 0

Hay-Bale Red Card

England 4

D.Barnes 46,89

J.Barnes 48,75

Fart Saved Pen

CHAPTER 10

Professional Footballers

The phone rang for about the fiftieth time that morning. Dad came in and spoke excitedly;

"That's sorted then. Northgate said that the FA have cleared it with FIFA that you can play both internationals and professionally despite your age."

The boy's debut for England had been like a dream and as a result, it seemed that every club in the country had been in touch, all except one.

With the game goalless at half-time, Northgate had made a double substitution pairing the youngest ever international players up front together. The England fans chanted;

"You don't know what you're doing!"

But the boos and jeers quickly turned to delight as the brothers combined with a fantastic one-two to allow Danny to walk around the keeper, Neville Dropall, before passing the ball into an empty net, whilst kissing his forearm in celebration where he had a fake Norchester City tattoo.

The England fans had barely stopped celebrating when Jimmy spotted Dropall off his line and lobbed the ball over him from all of 40 yards.

Jimmy added a superb free-kick to his tally to make it three-nil, which drew comparisons to the famous David Wickham Free kick versus Greece before Danny made it four-nil with a left foot pile-driver just before the full-time whistle.

If that wasn't enough drama Gary Hay-Bale lost his cool and picked up two yellow cards for cynical fouls on each of the boys to earn a red card and then he was heard to shout;

"I've got the best left foot in the world, that's right ME!" as he walked down the tunnel.

It was a particularly satisfying afternoon for the England Manager, Northgate, as the chants from the England fans changed to;

"You know exactly what you're doing!"

"Who wants to sign us then Dad?"

"Well lads," Dad replied, "you now have offers from all of the Premier League teams and even Norchester Town have been on the phone, but there is no way you are signing for them!"

"What about City?" both boys asked at once.

"No word yet I'm afraid," said Dad. Then the doorbell rang.

CHAPTER 11

Celia Whisk

Stood at the front door was world famous Chef and Norchester City F.C. owner Celia Whisk.

Whisk had made her fortune from recipe books and cooking shows for as long as Dad could remember, before investing in the team that she loved. This had been a dream come true for her and also for the fans.

"Where are they?" asked Celia.

Dad pointed to the front room where the boys were busy arguing over what to watch on YouTube when she walked in.

"Do you know who I am?" she said.

"Dads new girlfriend?" laughed Danny.

"NO!" said Dad and Celia Whisk in unison, neither of them laughing!

"This is Celia Whisk from Norchester City," Dad said.

"Let's be Havin you," joked Jimmy.

"No, let's be Havin you two!" replied Celia with a smile.

Celia explained that she had come on behalf of the manager and the board of the club and that they would very much like to sign Danny and Jimmy on a 10-year contract.

She had also spoken with Jimmy and Danny's football manager's and had agreed to loan one each of the Murphy brothers to their teams until they could find a replacement for the lads.

"Well I am happy boys – but it's your decision," said Dad. "Just had an email from Atletico Madrid, but you would have to learn the language," he added.

"No, No, No, Mamma Mia" laughed Jimmy in an Italian accent.

"Madrid are Spanish you muppet" bellowed Danny.

Jimmy and Danny asked if they could have a minute to discuss it, "alone please" they said to Dad, who begrudgingly left the room and stood outside with Celia.

Dad didn't think there was anything to discuss as the contract would set the boys up for life. He had insisted that their fortune would be held in trust until they were 18, when he hoped they would be old enough to make more sensible choices given that Jimmy had previously stated that if he ever won the lottery he would spend all his money on FIFA coins for his X-Box! Danny had said he would buy a sweet shop!

A minute passed before the boys shouted that it was ok for Celia and Dad to come back in. Five minutes later and after Celia had made a phone call, the lads were delighted that their three conditions had been met.

Condition one was that their nine-year-old cousin, Nicky would also be signed. Celia had not seen or heard of this lad but was happy as they now had three Barnes' signed and thought it would be great for shirt sales.

Condition two was that the Norchester City canteen would install a pick 'n' mix stand. With condition three being that the boys could have immediate access to a small part of their wages which would be paid to them in FIFA Coins. "Result" they said!

The next day the boys were introduced to the fans and the world's press by the Norchester City manager, Martin O'Malley and his assistant, Phil Peel. Danny was allocated the number 10 shirt, Jimmy number 7 and Nicky number 58, which the lads said was a coincidence as that's how old their Dad was! Dad was, in fact, twenty years younger but he didn't correct them.

CHAPTER 12

Promotion Race

The Barnes Boys quickly settled into life in the Championship, scoring a hatful of goals and lifting a struggling Norchester City side up the table to the brink of the play-off places. Celia was right about the shirt sales and the lads soon became crowd favourites.

Danny and Jimmy were paired up front with Nicky playing on either wing, though he preferred the right wing as Nicky thought his left foot was just for standing on. Nicky would typically swap with Danish winger Brian Loudmouth to provide the ammunition into the penalty area for his cousins to feast on. The opposition managers by now knew all about the Barnes's, but they could find no way of stopping them.

Norchester City went into their final league game against bottom of the league Rockpool knowing that all that was needed was a draw to ensure a place in the play-off finals.

As usual for home games, all three of the boys stayed with their Nana and Grandad in Norchester the night before the match so that they did not have to travel too far on the day of a game.

The boys were excited, too excited in fact and after persuading their Nana to let them sleep in the same room, it was 3 o'clock in the morning before the charge on the last iPad ran out, and 4 am before they were all asleep! It was hard to know if it was nerves from the match or the sugar rush from their midnight feast, that they had smuggled in, that had kept them awake.

Either way, by the time kick off came all three were yawning and stretching and could barely stay awake. The home crowd became restless as the usual attacks just did not happen and it came as no surprise when the bottom club took the lead on the stroke of halftime. Nicky made a tired challenge on the edge of his own area and from the resulting free-kick, Charlie Adams-Apple curled in a superb effort, leaving the City Keeper Davie Sea-Dog watching helplessly as the ball sped past him into the back of the City net.

In the dressing room, O'Malley lost his temper at halftime and asked his team what was wrong?

"You look like you have never played together," he bellowed. "Nicky where are the crosses, Danny, Jimmy, where's that pace, your skills, your desire?"

The boys knew the answer. They thought that they only needed a draw from the match and it was only bottom of the league after all. They had been complacent and thought that they just needed to turn up. But here was a Rockpool side who although already relegated were not going down without a fight.

Jimmy got his brother and cousin into a huddle in the toilets.

"Ok," he said, "we have underestimated Rockpool and Nana shouldn't have let us stay up so late. We need to wake up."

"I've got it, follow me," said Danny as he turned and went into the showers, placed the handle to cold, then walked in, still fully dressed!

"Just like the ice bucket challenge," he murmured, emerging dripping wet, freezing cold, but now fully awake. Danny knew that the icy cold water would wake them up. Jimmy and Nicky did the same and it worked a treat. A goal from Danny and Nicky's first Norchester City goal (a bullet header) sealed the win and ensured City would be in the Championship play-off's.

As the city team took a lap of honour around the stadium pitch, with the crowd showing particular appreciation for the three young superstars, the stadium tannoy boomed out the final day's results.

There was a huge cheer when it was announced that Norchester Town had lost, slipping down to third place in the league table, missing out on an automatic promotion place in the process.

Final Championship League Table

Team	Played	GD	Points
Oldcastle United	46	25	96
Southcoast F.C	46	22	88
Norchester Town	46	12	87
Midland Rovers	46	17	80
Norchester City	46	46	74
Teeside United	46	21	73

CHAPTER 13

Play-Off Semi-Final, First Leg

The Norchester City victory on the last day of the season meant that they overtook Teeside United, setting up a semi-final play-off clash with Midland Rovers. The first leg would be at City, with the decider away at Rovers.

The other semi-final would be between Norchester Town and Teeside United. Jimmy and Nicky had not stopped talking about the prospect of the first ever derby game against Town at Wembley. On the day of the first leg, Danny was unusually quiet. His Grandad asked him what was wrong as he was clearly not his usual self?

"Grandad," said Danny, "loads of my mates are Rovers fans, they will all hate me if we knock them out of the play-offs."

"Ah," replied Grandad, "is that why you are so quiet? I thought it was because Nana had let you stay up late again!"

Grandad thought for a moment and then spoke;

"Danny, if they are real mates then they will be happy for you. You have achieved something that they are all still dreaming of. They will think that if Danny can make it as a professional footballer then maybe we can do it to!"

Danny needn't have worried, his mates, Jimmy's mates and it seemed half of their school plus even some of their teachers, had all made the long journey for the away leg and were delighted to see both Danny and Jimmy before the game. Danny laughed when his headmistress, Mrs Hawkeye, asked for his autograph, but she wasn't joking!

The game itself was very scrappy and Midland Rovers were extremely physical, with some crunching tackles and many fouls committed.

Norchester City's passing game and speed advantage prevailed and saw them take a second-half lead with Nicky heading home Jimmy's far post cross which was enough to send the capacity crowd home happy enough.

However, in two-legged ties, a single goal advantage is often not enough, plus Rovers would have the advantage of their noisy home crowd for the second leg, meaning that the tie was far from over. There was no lap of honour from the team this time, as they recognised that only half the job was done and that many a team had won the first leg only to be beaten soundly in the second leg.

In the other semi-final, Norchester Town were beaten two goals to nil at Teeside United and were lucky that it was only two nil with Teeside missing a host of chances! It looked like only one of the Norchester teams would make it to Wembley.

Meanwhile up in the stands, with the ground now almost empty Dad looked at Grandad in disbelief as they marvelled in silence at what their sons and Grandsons had achieved in such a short space of time.

"I just hope they can handle the pressure," Dad exclaimed. Only time would tell.

CHAPTER 14

Play-Off Semi-Final, Second Leg

The second leg of the championship semi-final against Midland Rovers would be a 30,000 sell-out crowd, with the Norchester City fans snapping up their full allocation of 5,000 tickets.

Jimmy and Danny had asked if their Dad and Grandad would like to go in the Directors box as guests of Celia Whisk, but they agreed that they wanted to go in with the away fans as that was where the best atmosphere would be.

With only a one-nil advantage from the first leg the Norchester City manager Martin O'Malley knew he could not afford to go and simply defend, but with Danny, Nicky and Jimmy in the team there was no chance of that happening!

The speed at which City could break on the counter-attack was spectacular. Jimmy had tweeted earlier in the week that he was quicker than the Olympic sprinter Usain Bolt for a laugh, but Bolt had reacted and now wanted to race him at Wembley!

O'Malley's instruction to the team in the pre-match build-up was clear;

"Defend as a unit, and that includes you three! Then break in numbers and let's show the watching millions that we belong in the Premier League!"

The word millions stuck in Jimmy's head…… millions, there would be millions watching he thought, millions! What if he made a mistake, what if he missed a sitter, suddenly he felt his heart pounding……

"Come on Jimmy we've got a game to win," shouted Danny without a care in the world punching his brother playfully on the arm.

Danny had always been the more laid-back brother, Dad always told him that it came from being the second child.

"Whatever" Jimmy replied, waving his hand across his face like the wrestler John Cena, but inside Jimmy was more nervous than he had ever been and as well as his heart pounding he kept needing to go to the toilet, thankfully only for a wee!

The game started at one hundred miles an hour, Norchester City did indeed break in numbers and with speed, but whenever the ball came to Jimmy it seemed to bounce off him or he would take an extra touch and get tackled. Jimmy could hear his Dad saying to him;

"As a striker, it's your job to hold the ball up to give your defenders a break and to allow your teammates to get up to support the attack."

Just before halftime City broke but when Jimmy gave the ball away cheaply Rovers lumped it into the City box.

The City defender Fernando's headed clearance was poor, only making it as far as the edge of the area. The ball was poked back into the City box, then there was an almighty scramble with the ball eventually landing at the feet of the Rovers striker Francis who simply couldn't miss.

Championship Play Off Semi Final's Half Time Scores

Midland Rovers 1   Norchester City 0
Francis 44

1-1 on aggregate

Norchester Town 2   Teeside United 0
Wrong 12,38

2-2 on aggregate

CHAPTER 15

Play-Off Semi-Final,
Second Leg, Second Half

Jimmy trudged down the tunnel knowing that he had just cost his team a goal. Dad was always going on about why a striker needs to hold the ball up and now he knew why.

Suddenly a huge, towering figure stepped in front of him, blocking his path to the changing room. Jimmy looked up and up and up, expecting trouble, but what he saw was a familiar face, though it belonged to someone he had never actually met.

Usain Bolt had a smile that made you just want to smile with him. Despite just conceding an equaliser that was partly his fault, Jimmy could not help but grin back at Bolt as the Jamaican athlete towered over him.

"Hey man, you ready for that race now?" Bolt asked.

"I thought you were a United fan?" Jimmy replied.

Bolt laughed and countered;

"Not today Jimmy, today I am cheering for Norchester City as I want our race at Wembley, so don't let me down, big man!"

"I won't" replied Jimmy.

It suddenly dawned on Jimmy, 'I can't let him down, or the fans, my teammates, my mates, my Dad, my Grandad, my Cousin, ... my Brother!' We must beat Rovers!

O'Malley had told the recently recalled Murphy brothers to get stripped off.

"Jimmy, you're off," he said in his strong Irish accent.

"Wait" cried Jimmy "just give me ten minutes and I'll get us back into this" he pleaded whilst dropping to his knees and pretending to pray.

O'Malley thought about it looking at Jimmy, Danny and Nicky who all appeared to be staring back at him with eyes like a cute puppy dog. These kids had appeared from nowhere and dragged his team into the play-offs with the best run in the club's history. Could he really afford to sub them?

"OK, YOU HAVE TEN MINUTES," declared O'Malley in a now 'loud' Irish accent.

The Murphy brothers shrugged their shoulders and begrudgingly put their tracksuits back on, each muttering something that O'Malley couldn't quite hear.

The second half started with the same pace and ferocity as the first half. Time seemed to be racing by, at least for Jimmy. He looked up at the huge scoreboard which glowed brightly against the now dark night sky, 52 minutes gone and he hadn't touched the ball in the second half.

He saw the Murphy brothers stretching and then running up and down the line, eager to get on. Jimmy couldn't blame them he would feel exactly the same in their situation as they just wanted their chance to shine.

So why let this chance go by? he thought. I need the ball, I need the ball;

"Give me the ball," he said under his breath.

"Give me the ball!" he bellowed.

Hamburger heard his strikers' shout, having received the ball deep in his own half, he drilled it towards Jimmy who had taken up a good position in the centre circle. Jimmy dropped short to receive the pass, which also made sure that the Rovers defender could not nip in front of him to win the ball.

Jimmy knew that his first touch had deserted him tonight, so cleverly he decided not to touch the ball at all. As the ball sped towards him, he simply opened his legs at the last second and let the ball go through them, completely outwitting the Rovers defender. The no-touch turn had worked a treat and Jimmy raced clear of the Rovers defence towards the opposition goal. Now he was one on one and he could clearly see the whites of the keeper's eyes.

Jimmy was completely in control and now felt completely calm even though he was moving at top speed. There was no pounding heart and no need to go to the toilet.

He just had to decide would he slip it past the keeper, blast it, go around him, dink it……. so many choices. As it turned out he chose none of those! He passed……

CHAPTER 16

Hat-trick Hero

Jimmy was quick, maybe not as quick as his new pal Usain Bolt, but he was certainly amongst the quickest footballers in the country if not in the world!

His brother was also fast, as was his cousin. The pair moved at the speed of two formula 1 racing cars accelerating away from the start of a race to support Jimmy and to get any rebound from his shot. But Jimmy didn't shoot, he was completely in control and had created time and space to decide his next move. Out of the corner of his eye, he noticed both his brother and his cousin moving like lightning to support him.

It was then that Jimmy decided to completely unselfishly roll the ball to the side of the goalkeeper into the path of Danny and Nicky. It was Danny who arrived a fraction of a second earlier than Nicky, taking a touch before hammering the ball into the back of the Rovers net with his right foot, to send the Norchester City fans into a frenzy.

Danny ran to his adoring fans but pointed to his brother to signal that it was Jimmy's moment of genius that had set up the goal. Norchester City were back in front and now there was no looking back. Jimmy's nerves were a distant memory.

If Jimmy couldn't put a foot right in the first half, the second half was completely the opposite. Every touch he took was perfect, every turn came off just as he anticipated and when he was eventually subbed by O'Malley it was only so he and his brother could receive the applause of the travelling fans. Jimmy for his perfect second half Hat-trick (Right foot, Left foot, Header in that order) and Danny for his goal and excellent all-round performance.

The Murphy brothers got barely 3 minutes before the referee blew the final whistle. Today, there was no question of who would win the man of the match award, taking the ball home with him.

Championship Play Off Semi Final Full Time Scores

Midland Rovers 1

Francis 44

Norchester City 4

J.Barnes 60, 65, 72

D.Barnes 53

Norchester City win 5-1 on aggregate

Norchester Town 3

Wrong 12,38

W Ravioli OG 89

Teeside United 0

Norchester Town win 3-2 on aggregate

"Lads we've got Norchester Town in the Final" shouted Nicky as he poured a bottle of lemonade over Jimmy's head. Danny grabbed the bottle and took a swig, asking;

"How come we can't have champagne like the rest of the players?"

CHAPTER 17

Rivals

"Just how intense is the rivalry between Norchester City and Norchester Town?" asked Gary Vinegar.

"Well," replied Nicky, "it may not be the biggest derby game in the country, but it's the one that both sets of fans look for when the fixtures are released and it will be our first appearance in one so we really can't wait, especially as its at Wembley where we will get to smash them!"

Since Norchester City's semi-final victory over Rovers, the demand for interviews with the players (and in particular the Barnes trio) had been enormous.

The training ground was packed with fans just waiting to get a glimpse of the young stars. They seemed to love every minute, stopping to pose for selfies and to sign autographs.

The boys had become quite accustomed to working with the media. The media seemed to love interviewing them to, especially as the answers the lads gave were somewhat different to most footballers. There was no 'take every game as it comes' or 'there are no easy games'. Instead there were lots of 'I'll mug him off' and 'nah we will stuff them!'

When tickets for the final went on sale the queues were the longest that City had ever seen and Norchester City sold their full ticket allocation in a day.

It was the same story in Norchester Town, no one it seemed wanted to miss out on this final. The boys had managed to secure enough tickets for their families, friends, former grassroots team-mates and also Nicky's new girlfriend. The boys had discovered that their new-found fame had made them very popular with girls all of a sudden, though Jimmy and Danny had decided to concentrate on their football, a wise move thought their Dad.

Meanwhile, Norchester Town were planning how they were going to stop the three Barnes Boys. Nicky saying they were going to 'smash' them at Wembley had really annoyed the Town manager, players and fans.

The Town manager, Bertie Bassett, had decided that the best way would, in fact, be to 'smash them!'

"Kick them and kick them hard! Right lads?" shouted Bassett, pointing at the picture of the Barnes trio that was pinned to a dart-board on the dressing room wall at the Norchester Town training ground.

"Do anything you need to do to stop them, but make sure that you don't get seen by the ref or the linesman, we won't win if we get sent off, right?"

The Norchester Town team nodded and agreed that it was the best way to stop the boys and that a good boot would see these 'kids' being carried off injured. Town defender Gary Bannister smashed his clenched fist into his hand, saying "Right Boss!"

"Do that and we win the match!" shouted Bassett.

"Don't worry boss, we get the message," replied the Town skipper John Smelly.

But whilst Norchester Town were planning their assault on the boys, over at Norchester City, Martin O'Malley was sat in his office with a worried look on his face.

He picked up the phone and asked his secretary to send up the three Barnes boys. When the secretary opened the door to the players' lounge, she found Jimmy shouting;

"mercy, mercy" as Danny and Nicky were lying on top of him punching, tickling, squeezing and booting him.

"Boys, the Gaffer wants to see you in his office now," she said. No one answered, or even looked up…………

"NOW!" she shouted.

The boys went upstairs to the gaffer's office, wondering what the boss wanted to discuss.

"Sit down," he said, gesturing them towards the sofa in the corner of the room. The boys sat.

"What is it Gaffer?" asked Nicky.

"I'm worried, worried about the game, well not the game, but what Norchester Town may have lined up for you three," explained O'Malley.

"Boss," answered Jimmy, "we can handle anything they throw at us."

"Yeah" added Danny, "we have been kicked, pulled, scratched, rugby tackled and even bitten ever since we started playing so we are used to it."

"Danny, do you remember when that kid pulled your shorts down?" laughed Jimmy.

"Besides," said Nicky, "if they want to try and kick us then they have to catch us first!"

"Let's just play our football," added Jimmy, "we can handle ourselves."

O'Malley looked at the boys, they were just 8, 9 and 10 years old. He could see from their bedraggled appearance that they had been fighting with each other.

"I'm sure you can," he said, "I'm sure you can," he repeated again, this time with a big smile on his face.

CHAPTER 18

Play-Off Final, Wembley, Team Line Up's

Town

Shay Taken

Gary Bannister

John Smelly (C)

Daryl Brazil

Ian Wrong

Mark Toobright

Walter Melon

Don Trump

David Gold

Dwight Cork

Bobby Fouler

City

Davie Sea-Dog

Ryan Fernando

Frank Hamburger (C)

Chris P. Bacon

Nicky Barnes

Danny Barnes

Jimmy Barnes

Bryan Loudmouth

Patrick Voila

Paul Wince

Dennis Cubcamp

Substitutes

Town
Jack Pott
Yoyo Turnip
Owen Michaels
Mark Skid
Casper Cycle (G)

City
Reg Vardy
Murphy
Murphy
Alan Sheardrop
Peter Shrimpton (G)

Manager

Bertie Bassett
Barry Kidding (A)

Martin O'Malley
Phil Peel

Officials

Referee
Assistant Referee
Assistant Referee
4th Official

Mike Battenburg
Willy Waite
Tim Burr
Rick O'Shea

CHAPTER 19

Play-Off Final, Wembley, Formalities

The atmosphere at Wembley was electric, it seemed to be almost bouncing as the 80,000 supporters chanted and shouted.

'Come on City' ....

Could be heard coming from the Norchester City end, as well as;

'3 times, weeer gonna beat you 3 times, weeer gonna beat you 3 times'

as a reference to the fact that Norchester City had already beaten Norchester Town home and away this season. The Norchester Town fans were singing;

'Norchester Town till I die, I'm Norchester Town till I die, I know I am, I'm sure I am I'm Norchester Town till I die'.

"Phones away now," demanded O'Malley, just as Jimmy was listening to a good luck message from the England Manager Bobby Northgate.

At the end of the message there was a muffled voice which Jimmy thought was Harry Breville, saying that he still wanted the kits back. Jimmy killed the call, turned off the phone and pulled on his Norchester City kit along with the rest of his team-mates.

The boys were desperate to get onto the pitch and to get playing. It seemed like an age to them before the game eventually kicked off because of the formalities which take place at Wembley Finals.

Firstly, there was the respect handshake between the two teams, which the boys did not think was very respectful. The Norchester Town players seemed to be trying to squeeze the boy's hands really tightly and they were also taunting them.

"I'm going to break your legs!" whispered John Smelly.

"Watch your Back!" hissed Daryl Brazil and;

"Come near me and you'll be sorry!" added Gary Bannister.

"Friendly lot!" said Nicky sarcastically.

The Norchester City mascot did manage to fool the Norchester Town striker Ian Wrong though, by pretending to shake his hand then pulling it away at the last moment much to Wrong's annoyance.

The players then met and shook the hand of Prince William, with Danny asking him how his Nan was, much to the Prince's amusement, replying that she was a massive fan of the boys!

Then there was the National Anthem to sing and as the boys belted out the words Nicky and Danny giggled at Jimmy's out of tune singing!

Finally, there was the coin toss to decide who kicked off and at which end they would line up. It was at this point that the boys noticed who the referee was …… Mike Battenburg!

"Oh no," blurted Nicky, "he didn't give us anything last time he refereed our match!" Battenburg had been the official for City's away win against Trumpton some weeks earlier, with both Martin O'Malley and the Trumpton manager, Louis van Goal, both commenting that the referee should have produced more cards.

Norchester Town won the toss and decided to attack the end where the Norchester City fans were assembled, meaning they would attack the goal in front of their own fans in the second half.

"Let's make sure that's the only thing they win this afternoon," demanded City captain Frank Hamburger as they had their pre-match huddle.

"Remember the game plan, get the ball to the boys and they will do the rest" he added.

The referee, Battenburg, blew the whistle, with Norchester City kicking off. Danny touched the ball to Jimmy who played it back to Frank Hamburger. Hamburger floated the ball out to the right wing where Nicky controlled it instantly, setting off on a penetrating run, only to be halted by a blatant shoulder charge from Smelly. It was surely a yellow card, but Battenburg wagged his finger and gave him a stern warning.

"This is going to be a long afternoon," sighed the boys Grandad up in the stands.

CHAPTER 20

Play-Off Final, Wembley, First Half

Grandad felt every tackle, foul and kick. It was his Grandchildren out there after all.

"Ref, they need some protection!" he shouted from the stands as Norchester Town committed what must have been the twentieth foul on the boys, despite the fact that only 5 minutes had been played.

"That referee Claxenburger needs to get his book out!" he added.

O'Malley was up on his feet pleading with the referee to protect his youngsters. He shouted to Bertie Bassett;

"They are only kids Bertie, what are you playing at?"

"Shut Up O'Malley" he bellowed back. "It's a man's game, perhaps you should bring on some older players," he added as he gestured towards the Murphy brothers sat on the bench.

The Norchester Town players spent the rest of the first half kicking, pulling, poking and even punching Jimmy, Nicky and Danny, mostly without being seen by the referee or either of the linesmen. When they did see an incident all the Norchester Town players seemed to receive was a telling off!

"I bet they have been told not to spoil the game with an early sending off," said the boys Dad.

"But it is spoiling the game," replied Amelia, "it's spoiling it for me anyway!"

There was a certain irony in Amelia's statement, as she would usually be the one kicking, pulling, poking and punching her brother and sometimes her cousins, but it was alright for her to do it, in her mind anyway.

Norchester Town made no attempt to play any football, they just lumped the ball forward playing everything long. City, on the other hand, played one-touch football and tried to move the ball quickly, 'pass, pass, pass, great pass', but it would end with oooohhhh that's gotta hurt, as one of the boys would be clattered into from behind.

Battenburg blew the whistle to signal the end of the first half of one of the dirtiest play-off finals that the pundits could remember.

"Good work boys the plans working," declared Frank Hamburger to the three Barnes boys as they pretended to limp off back towards the changing rooms.

Championship Play-Off Final Half Time Score

Norchester Town 0   Norchester City 0

Yellow Cards

Bannister

Smelly

CHAPTER 21

Play-Off Final, Wembley,
Dressing Rooms

The Norchester City players took their seats in the dressing room ready to listen to O'Malley.

"They are getting slaughtered out there," he whispered to his captain,
"I'll make a change."

"No Boss, replied Hamburger, "this is part of the plan!"

Frank Hamburger explained that after the 'respect handshake,' the Norchester City team had gone into a huddle where he had outlined to the team that the boys were going to get 'roughed up' by the Norchester Town players. Danny had piped up saying;

"Don't worry skipper, haven't you ever seen the Rocky films?"

Hamburger had looked puzzled. Jimmy explained that in Rocky 4, Rocky lets the big Russian boxer beat him up so badly, but at the same time he was tiring himself out. It looked like Rocky was beaten, but then he surprised the Russian boxer by suddenly springing an amazing counter attack on him.

"So, we do the same to Norchester Town, let them kick us, we'll limp about, they will get tired and bang we will have them in the second half!" explained Jimmy.

"Genius," replied Hamburger, "but I wouldn't like to be in your shoes."

"Nah they wouldn't fit" replied Danny with a puzzled look on his face.

Meanwhile, in the Norchester Town dressing room the players were grinning, but looking very hot and tired!

"I wouldn't be surprised to see them all subbed," said Bassett to his players.

"It's working a treat," added Smelly with a big grin on his face.

"They have hardly had a touch," Bannister squealed excitedly.

"We have got this in the bag," laughed Brazil.

The Norchester Town physio was busy repairing all the cuts and bruises that the Norchester Town defenders and midfielders had sustained when kicking the Barnes boys. There were so many that he ran out of plasters!

Bassett looked somewhat shocked as his team took to the field when he saw that the Norchester City team were already out on the Wembley turf. What shocked him even more was that the three Barnes boys were not only lined up ready to play but were playing what looked like headers and volleys with Prince William and a ball boy like they didn't have a care in the world!

CHAPTER 22

Play-Off Final, Wembley, Second Half

Norchester Town kicked off the second half and immediately played the ball backwards before it was once again launched deep into the City half. Norchester City continued to try and play football and Norchester Town continued to do anything but!

O'Malley decided it was time for a tactical change just ten minutes into the second half, bringing on the veteran striker Alan Sheardrop for midfielder Patrick Voila as the ball was not going anywhere near the midfield area, at least when Norchester Town had it. Sheardrop gave Jimmy the instruction to play in the hole behind the strikers leaving him and Danny up front.

But the drama quickly unfolded at the Norchester City end. Once again Town played the ball long, but when the City goalkeeper Davie Sea-Dog came to catch the ball the Norchester Town striker Ian Wrong clattered into him. The ball ran lose to his strike partner Mark Toobright who rolled the ball into the empty net sending the Norchester Town fans into ecstasy.

Sea-Dog was stretchered off unconscious and Martin O'Malley protested so much about the obvious foul that he was sent off, having to sit in the stands for the rest of the game.

But the goal stood, Norchester Town were leading the play-off final.

Bertie Bassett sang;

"Cheerio, cheerio, cheerio" to O'Malley as he walked to the stands.

City brought on their substitute keeper, Peter Shrimpton to replace Sea-Dog.

Norchester Town 1   Norchester City 0

Toobright 57

To make matters worse for City, Alan Sheardrop had not warmed up thoroughly enough and he winced with pain as he pulled his hamstring bending down to do up his shoelace. The Norchester City assistant manager, Phil Peel, looked to the bench, the Murphy brothers were the obvious choice, but it would leave City with no more substitutions.

"Murphy, you're on" bellowed Peel.

"Which one?" they both said at once.

"I don't care, just one of you get on that pitch!" shouted Peel.

The second half was not going to plan for City and Town were still kicking and fouling the boys but were noticeably starting to tire.

"Come on Rocky its time!" Danny bellowed to Nicky. Nicky sensed his moment as the ball was played into his feet by the city centre back, Ryan Fernando, almost on the halfway line out on the right wing. With his back to goal, Nicky could feel the breath of the Town defender Gary Bannister down his neck. But Bannister was tight, too tight and as he went to kick Nicky up into the air Nicky flicked the ball and rolled past Bannister, who fell to the floor partly with tiredness from all the kicking but mainly with embarrassment.

Nicky raced down the wing. Jimmy and Danny and one of the Murphy's shot off at speed to try and get in the box ready for the cross. As Nicky got to the edge of the area, he saw that the Town goalkeeper, Shay Taken, was creeping off his line expecting a cross and leaving his near post exposed.

The ball was in the back of the Town goal within the blink of an eye as Nicky had swerved the ball with the outside of his right foot high into the roof of the net beating the Town goalie on his front post.

It was easily the best goal Nicky had ever scored and also the most important. Rather than celebrate excessively Nicky ran to the goal, grabbed the ball and sprinted back to the centre circle with his arm raised shouting;

"Now let's win this match and get City back to the Premier League!"

Meanwhile, in the crowd, a very proud voice was shouting "that's my brother!"

Norchester Town 1   Norchester City 1
Toobright 57   N.Barnes 78

City were now full of confidence and passed the ball first time keeping possession for what seemed like 5 minutes, although it was only thirty seconds. Meanwhile the City fans cheered 'Olé' every time a pass was made.

Murphy, Danny and Jimmy linked up and played Nicky in again as he tore through the fatigued Norchester Town defenders like a knife through butter. There seemed no way they were going to stop him, at least legally, then Bannister cynically body-checked him, sending Nicky flying. Battenburg blew his whistle but his cards stayed in his pocket which was lucky for Bannister as he had already been booked.

Danny grabbed the ball for the free kick which was 25 yards from goal but whispered to Jimmy;

"Bro this is perfect for a right footer but let's do the free kick we practised."

Battenburg blew his whistle, this time to indicate that City could take the free kick. Danny approached the ball as if he was going to strike it left-footed and then did a summersault over the top of the ball in a bid to confuse the wall and keeper, leaving Jimmy to strike the ball right footed.

The ball rose up and over the wall curling and dipping as time seemed to stand still. Shay Taken dived to his left as the ball struck the underside of the crossbar and bounced down on to the line …… but Jimmy had hit the ball with such power that the ball bounced back up off the line before hitting the underside of the crossbar again, this time hitting the back of the crossbar and nestling in the back of the Town net.

Norchester Town 1

Toobright 57

Norchester City 2

N.Barnes 78

J.Barnes 84

Unlike Nicky, Jimmy did celebrate, running to the Norchester City crowd behind the goal, ripping his shirt off to reveal a t-shirt with the slogan 'why is it always me' which he had borrowed from his new Italian pal, Mario Spaghetti.

Norchester City just had to hold out for 6 minutes plus injury time, of which there would be quite a lot, 8 minutes in fact as the fourth official, Rick O'Shea, held up the board.

The Norchester Town fans roared and urged their team to pump it forward, but for once Town passed the ball and kept it on the floor.

The Norchester City defence seemed so surprised that Town were actually playing football that they didn't notice Ian Wrong racing clear and suddenly finding himself one on one with City's substitute goalkeeper Peter Shrimpton. His speed instantly took him around the goalkeeper leaving Shrimpton little option but to bring him down. It was a blatant penalty and Shrimpton was sent off ...... Disaster.

City had no subs left to use, were down to ten men, had no goalkeeper, their manager had been sent off and now they were facing extra time with a man less than their bitter rivals Norchester Town!

"**DOOMED**" shouted Grandad.

CHAPTER 23

Play-Off Final, Wembley, Added Time

Martin O'Malley was shouting;

"Barnes, Barnes, Barnes" as loud as he could from his seat in the stands.

Phil Peel, the Norchester City assistant manager, was trying to listen to the instruction of his manager, but the noise from the capacity crowd was deafening. He could make out O'Malley mouthing 'Barnes' which was fine except there were three of them!

Frank Hamburger had seen all the boys play in goal during training and would have been happy to put any of them in, but Shrimpton's goalie shirt was pretty big. The Dutch legend, Dennis Cubcamp spoke;

"Well, Jimmy's the biggest," so they went with Jimmy.

The goal looked enormous with Jimmy in it and the goalkeeper's jersey looked enormous on Jimmy!

Gary Vinegar remarked;

"Imagine what it would have looked like on his brother!"

Ian Wrong was the designated Norchester Town penalty taker and as he had won the spot kick there was no question who would take the penalty.

Score and there would almost certainly be extra time. Miss and he would surely send Norchester City into the Premier League, which was the worst possible scenario for a Town player.

Danny approached Jimmy to offer him some advice, but Jimmy had watched Ian Wrong take penalties numerous times on the Championship TV show and also in real life. However, this didn't really help as Jimmy knew that sometimes Wrong put them to the goalkeepers left, sometimes he put them to the goalkeeper's right and sometimes he just blasted them up the middle.

Jimmy decided he would guess and as it turned out he got lucky. Wrong struck the ball low and hard to his left, Jimmy guessed correctly, diving to his right and tipping the ball with his fingertips on to the post and out for a corner. The Norchester City fans went wild and the players all jumped on Jimmy.

But City's celebrations were short-lived as Battenburg blew hard on his whistle. Battenburg seemed to be smiling, almost as if he knew the cameras were on him, as he explained to the Town and City players that Jimmy had moved off his line before the ball was kicked, meaning that the penalty would have to be re-taken!

Could Jimmy get lucky again?

Wrong decided he would again take the penalty. Now the pressure had reached fever pitch. He stepped up and this time decided to go for pure power blasting the ball right up the centre. Jimmy didn't get lucky this time and the ball sailed over his legs as he dived to the left.

Norchester Town 2   Norchester City 2

Toobright 57   N.Barnes 78

Wrong 90 + 5   J.Barnes 84

Town were happy to settle for extra time, after all they now had an extra man. There were barely 2 minutes to go and they tried to waste every second of it. But they were tired, really tired, having been chasing the three Barnes boys all around the huge Wembley pitch, kicking them at every opportunity.

City easily won the ball back deep in their own half. Fernando brought the ball out of defence, as the referee Battenburg looked at his watch, 1 minute to go.

Chris P. Bacon played it short to Hamburger, who in turn passed to Danny on the halfway line, who turned and spotted Nicky making a run down the right wing. His pass was inch perfect and Nicky sprinted towards the corner flag only to find his path to the by-line blocked by two defenders.

Nicky wanted to curl the ball in with his right foot, but as the defenders blocked that option he instead did a 'Cruyff turn' taking the ball back on to his left foot allowing him to whip in a superb delivery to the back post.

Nicky would never usually have used his left foot but he had spent hours practising and he had found it had got stronger and stronger.

"Wow," he cried out loud amazed at his own delivery.

Murphy met the cross and headed it back towards the penalty spot where Danny had raced to, anticipating that it was where he needed to be.

Danny realised he had slightly misjudged his run, he had arrived too early and now the ball was dropping behind him.

Up in the stands, his Dad knew just what was about to happen. He had seen it before many times, as the lads were always practising their spectacular shots in the garden. However, more often than not, especially in the early days, the ball had ended up in the neighbour's garden!

"Go on son," he whispered quietly to himself.

In an instant, Danny turned his body so his back was facing towards the goal. Then he launched himself into the air as the crowd all seemed to simultaneously stand up in anticipation.

Jimmy, Nicky and the rest of the players looked on. Time seemed to stand still once more as Danny hung in the air and then executed the most perfect overhead kick ever seen at Wembley.

The shot sped towards the Town goal and even Shay Taken seemed to admire it as the ball rocketed into the top corner in the blink of an eye.

Danny picked himself up from the floor and ran the entire length of the pitch, with his teammates in hot pursuit, before sliding on his chest in celebration right in front of the Norchester Town fans. There was no way that the rest of the players were catching him, that is until he finally came to a stop!

What followed was a new world record for the biggest 'pile on' ever at a football game as the entire Norchester City team, subs, coaching staff and even the mascot jumped on to celebrate.

Somewhere at the bottom of the pile were the youngest ever goal-scorers in a Wembley final. Battenburg blew his whistle one last time …… but this time it was to signal the end of the match!

Norchester City were back in the Premier League!

Norchester Town 2
Toobright 57
Wrong 90 + 5

Norchester City 3
N.Barnes 78
J.Barnes 84
D.Barnes 90 + 8

The City Captain, Hamburger, insisted that he and the boys lift the trophy together. As they descended the Wembley steps, there at the bottom waiting for Jimmy was a familiar smiling face.

"Now let's race," said Bolt.

Score settled! Back in the changing rooms, there was no sign of the celebrations stopping. The boys were hurled in the air by the rest of their team-mates.

Bobby Northgate sat at home having watched the big match on his huge widescreen TV with his assistant Harry Breville, who was still clutching a small piece of paper.

The TV was showing the Norchester City celebrations which had now progressed to the changing rooms, with the boys being repeatedly thrown in the air.

"Don't injure them we've got Germany in a week!" shouted Northgate at the TV.

But that's another story!

The End

Printed in Great Britain
by Amazon